THE WORLD'S BIGGEST BOGEY

Steve Hartley is a sensible man. He has a sensible job, a sensible family, lives in a sensible house and drives a sensible car. But underneath it all, he longs to be silly. There have been occasional forays into silliness: Steve has been a football mascot called Desmond Dragon, and has tasted World Record success himself – taking part in both a mass yodel and a mass yo-yo. But he wanted more, and so his alter ego – Danny Baker Record Breaker – was created. Steve lives in Lancashire with his wife and teenage daughter.

You can find out more about Steve
on his extremely silly website:
www.stevehartley.net

STEVE HARTLEY

DANNY BAKER

RECORD BREAKER

THE WORLD'S
BIGGEST BOGEY

ILLUSTRATED BY KATE PANKHURST

MACMILLAN CHILDREN'S BOOKS

First published 2010 by Macmillan Children's Books
a division of Macmillan Publishers Limited
20 New Wharf Road, London N1 9RR
Basingstoke and Oxford
Associated companies throughout the world
www.panmacmillan.com

ISBN 978-0-330-50916-9

Text copyright © Steve Hartley 2010
Illustrations copyright © Kate Pankhurst 2010

5 7 9 8 6

A CIP catalogue record for this book is available from
the British Library.

Printed and bound by CPI Group (UK) Ltd, Croydon, CR0 4YY

For Rosie

Three hundred and forty-seven megazigzillion thanks to:

Connie, the Best Daughter in the World, whose love of records inspired the original idea.

Natascha Biebow, Sara Grant and Sara O'Connor for having the Best Idea in the World when they put together the SCBWI *Undiscovered Voices 2008* anthology.

Finally to three women who all love Danny as much as I do:
Sarah Manson, the Best Agent in the World, for knocking my writing into shape and expertly steering the Steve Hartley ship.
Emma Young, the Best Editor in the World, for plunging so enthusiastically into Danny's world of silliness.
And most of all to my wife, Louise, the Best Critic in the World, for so many Ace ideas, and for telling me when I'm funny, but more importantly, when I'm *not* funny.

This is entirely a work of fiction and any resemblance
to the real world is purely coincidental.

The Toxic Toes

WARNING!
THIS STORY
MAY CONTAIN
SILLINESS

Bogey

To the Manager
The Great Big Book of World Records
London

Dear Sir

I have been collecting bogeys from my nose
for the last two years. I have stuck them all
together to make one enormous bogey. It
measures 5.3 cm in diameter and weighs 3.6 g.
Here is a photograph of me holding the bogey.
Is this a record?

Yours faithfully
Danny Baker
(Aged nine and a bit)

me and my bogey ↑

ARE YOU A RECORD
BREAKER ?

Dear Danny Baker

Thank you for your letter about your big
bogey. I am sorry to tell you that it is not a
record.

Ronald Ramsbottom of Rawtenstall, Lancashire,
is the Individual Bogey world-record holder.
He was the All-England Nose-picking Champion
for thirteen straight years, from 1982 to 1994.
Unfortunately, in 1995 he chopped off his
right index finger trying to unblock a jammed
electric pencil sharpener. Ronald entered the
championship that year using his left index
finger, but came ninth. He retired, and now
picks his nose only for fun. His collected
bogeys measured 47 cm in diameter, and weighed
2.51 kg.

As a matter of interest, the biggest Team Bogey ever created was one that measured 5.1 m in diameter and weighed 3,198.7 kg. It took six years of continuous nose-picking by 467 boys from a school in Chichibu in Japan. On the day they decided to stop picking their noses, they invited their headmaster to add the final bogey. Tragically, just as he put his finger up his nose, a freak gust of wind started the ball rolling. The headmaster and fifteen of the boys were squashed to death. Thirty-one other pupils had to go to hospital. All of which goes to show that great care must be taken when attempting to break *any* world record.

Best wishes
Eric Bibby
Keeper of the Records

'Bad luck, Danny,' said his best friend Matthew Mason. He handed the letter back to Danny and continued tying up the laces on his football boots. 'Imagine being killed by a giant bogey. Gross.'

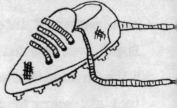

'Yeah,' agreed Danny. He pulled his green goalkeeper's shirt over his head and tucked it into his black shorts. He sighed and gazed dreamily into space. 'I was going to have my bogey mounted on a wooden stand and present it to Penleydale Museum. They'd have put it in a small glass case with a sign

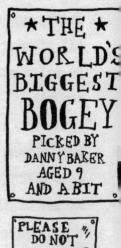

★ THE ★ WORLD'S BIGGEST BOGEY PICKED BY DANNY BAKER AGED 9 AND A BIT

PLEASE DO NOT TOUCH

saying THE WORLD'S BIGGEST BOGEY, PICKED BY DANNY BAKER, AGED NINE AND A BIT.' Danny sighed again. 'I'd have to pick my nose for years to make a bogey 47 centimetres in diameter.'

'You could just carry on anyway until you get there,' suggested Matthew.

'No point now,' grumbled Danny. 'Natalie used the bogey to play fetch with next door's dog and, instead of bringing it back, he ate it.'

'Gross! I'm surprised your sister wanted to touch the bogey in the first place.'

'She thought it was a rubber ball.' Danny grinned. 'She spent all afternoon washing her hands when she found out what it *really* was! Come on, let's go and beat the Snickwell Alleycats.'

With the studs on their boots clicking an upbeat

rhythm on the floor, Danny's team, the Coalclough Sparrows, walked out of the changing rooms to do just that, by four goals to nil.

'Well done, Danny,' said his dad when they got home from the game. 'You haven't let a goal in all season. If you carry on like this you're going to be better than I was.'

'I doubt it, Dad!'

Danny looked around at the shelves and glass display cabinets crammed with medals, trophies  and caps. The walls of his dad's study were so full of photographs and certificates that Danny could barely see what colour the wall underneath was painted. Danny's dad had been the Best

Goalkeeper in the World Ever. He played more times for his country, won more medals, played in more games and let in fewer goals than anyone else had ever done in the history of football. He even

had a Special Certificate from the Great Big Book of World Records.

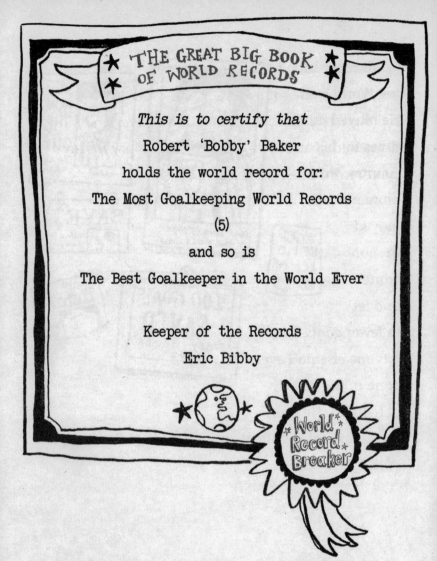

THE GREAT BIG BOOK
OF WORLD RECORDS

This is to certify that
Robert 'Bobby' Baker
holds the world record for:
The Most Goalkeeping World Records
(5)
and so is
The Best Goalkeeper in the World Ever

Keeper of the Records
Eric Bibby

World
Record
Breaker

Danny read the certificate for the umpteenth time.
'One day I'll be the best in the world at something,
Dad, just like you.'

His dad smiled. 'You're the best in the world to me, Danny,' he said.

That's not the same, thought Danny. He scratched his head vigorously. Time to try for my next record attempt.

Nits

Dear Mr Bibby

Last night my mum found 109 head lice on my head. Is this a record? When they checked, my mum and dad had them too. And my sister Natalie discovered that she was simply crawling with nits! She wasn't pleased, because she was just about to go to the school disco with her best friends Kaylie and Kylie.

a nit

We managed to collect fifty-seven more head lice, making a total of 166.
I have stuck them all on the bottom of this page as proof. Could this be a family record?

natalie

I hope it is, because it might make Nats feel better to know that she didn't miss the disco for nothing.

And she might stop trying to pull my ears off every time she sees me.

Yours sincerely
Danny Baker

THE
*GREAT
BIG
BOOK OF
WORLD
RECORDS

ARE YOU A RECORD
BREAKER ?

Dear Danny Baker

Thank you for the enquiry about your attempt
on the Most Head-lice world record, which I'm
sorry to tell you was unsuccessful.

This record is held by Arthur Grimley, a hermit
from Thornton Watlass in Yorkshire. He lived
alone in a cave on the North Yorkshire Moors
for forty-one years, and never washed in all
that time. His hair and beard reached down to
just above his knees. Whenever ramblers went
near his cave, he used to shout rude words at
them and jump up and down pulling faces. If
this didn't scare them away, he used to pull
his pants down and show them his bottom. I
imagine he had the dirtiest bottom in the world
too, but as far as I know no one dared to check!

One day, Arthur slipped on some ice outside his cave, and luckily was found soon after by some ramblers. He went to hospital and was washed and deloused. They counted 8,433 head lice, as well as 169 fleas. (This isn't a record. The most fleas ever counted on one person is 17,325.)

The record number of head lice ever collected from one family is 58,971. This record is held by the fifteen members of the Pickle family of West Virginia, USA.

Bad luck once again. Perhaps you should buy your sister a present and say you are sorry. Or buy yourself a hat with earmuffs. Sisters are just no fun are they?

Best wishes
Eric Bibby
Keeper of the
Records

The Pickle family W. Virginia

Danny lay in bed that morning, reading Mr Bibby's letter. He sighed with disappointment.

'Danny!' shouted his mum from downstairs. 'Get up, now!'

He got out of bed, yawned, stretched and scratched his tummy. He was wearing socks and trainers, and a pair of extremely grubby underpants. Danny had been wearing the same pants for six months, but so far his mum hadn't realized, because he'd been putting a clean pair in the wash bin every day.

He'd been doing the same with his socks.

Natalie appeared at his open bedroom door and stared at him with a strange mixture of triumph and disgust on her face.

'I'm telling Mum,' she sneered.

'Aw, don't, Nat,' begged Danny. 'She'll go ballistic.'

'You're revolting.'

'I'm just trying to break a world record.'

Natalie pulled a face. 'Which one? The Dirtiest Underpants?'

'No,' replied Danny truthfully, although he realized that he *could* try for that record, if he didn't break the one he was *actually* going for. 'It's a secret.'

'Fine, don't tell me then.' Natalie smirked. 'Mum!'

Danny quickly pulled on his jeans. 'I'll tidy your bedroom,' he offered desperately.

Natalie considered this for a moment, but then yelled, 'Mum!' again.

'I'll ask Matthew to do your maths homework for the next two weeks.'

'*Mum!*'

'What do you want, Natalie?' shouted Mum from downstairs. 'I've got the vacuum cleaner in pieces on the living-room floor.'

Danny pleaded with his eyes.

'Have you seen –' yelled Natalie. She grinned at her brother – 'my hairbrush?'

'No, I haven't,' answered Mum. 'Your bedroom's such a mess, I'm not surprised you've lost it.'

'It'll be tidy by tonight, don't worry.' Natalie glared menacingly at her brother. 'Won't it, Danny?'

'I promise. I'll do it after the game this afternoon.'

'And I won't have to do any maths homework for two weeks?'

'No.'

'OK then.' She stuck her tongue out at him, and went downstairs.

Danny sighed with relief and finished getting dressed. He picked up his football-kit bag and set off for school. The Coalclough Sparrows were going to play Crawshaw Cougars in the semi-final of the Penleydale Schools Cup.

Danny had another great game in goal, and the Sparrows won two–nil.

'We're in the Final!' cried Matthew, rubbing his hair dry with a large Walchester United towel. He and

Danny were getting changed after the match. 'It's fantastic!'

'Who do you think we'll play?' asked Danny. He hadn't had a shower, and was already dressed.

'It doesn't matter. We're playing so well, we can beat anybody.' Matthew threw the towel into his bag. 'Dan, why don't you ever have a shower after a game? Are you trying to break another record?'

'Yeah,' answered Danny, 'I've got a couple of things brewing actually. I didn't realize breaking world records would be so difficult. My Head-lice record attempt didn't even come close.'

'So *you're* the one who's given everyone nits.'

'Yeah.' Danny smiled proudly. 'It was me.'

'What's this new record you're working on then?'

'I'm going to try for the Spottiest Bum in the world. I've not washed my bum or changed my underpants now for nearly six months. That's why I never have a shower after a game.'

'*Six months?*' gasped Matthew. 'Gross!'

'Yeah, it's going really well – my bum is covered

in spots. I'm going to have to count them soon and write to Mr Bibby at the Great Big Book of World Records, because it really hurts when I sit down.'

'I'll bet it does,' said Matthew.

'How are you going to count them?'

Danny tried to look at his bottom over his shoulder, and then bent over to peer at it between his legs. 'I'm not sure. Use a mirror, I suppose. No, wait – you're ace at maths! Why don't you count them for me?'

'No way!'

'That reminds me. Nat the Brat was going to snitch about my underpants. I promised you'd do her maths homework for the next two weeks if she kept her mouth shut. Will you?'

Matthew rolled his eyes. 'Yeah, go on then. But I bet it'll be the first time Nat the Numbskull ever gets ten out of ten for her maths homework.'

'Thanks, Matt. By the way, I'm working on another record attempt too, just in case my spotty bum isn't a world-beater.'

'What?'

'I'm going for the Smelliest Feet record.'

Matthew stared at Danny's feet. 'Cool. How are you going to do it?'

'I've not changed my socks for six months.'

'Double-gross! That's a hundred and eighty days! I put on a clean pair every day!'

Danny beamed. 'I know – great, isn't it! And for the last six weeks I've not taken my shoes off except to put my football boots on.'

'Triple-gross! Not even at night, in bed?' asked Matthew.

'No,' replied Danny. 'If my mum finds out she'll go mad. I sit toasting my toes in front of the fire as much as I can. The rest of the time I keep my feet wrapped in a blanket.'

'They must be *really* sweaty by now,' said

Matthew. Danny could see he was impressed.

'But not sweaty enough,' said Danny. 'When people can smell them with my shoes on, that's when they'll be ready.'

Matthew leaned over Danny's feet and sniffed.

'Not yet,' he said.

'No, not yet,' agreed Danny.

Spot on the Bot

Dear Mr Bibby

It's me again. I have got 207 spots on my bottom. Is this a record? I've sent a photograph of my bottom as proof. My best friend, Matthew, who took the photo, says it's the most awesome thing he's ever seen. To

(207 spots (my bum)

get my bottom in this state, I didn't take off my underpants for over six months. I would have gone on longer, but my underpants had turned green and there were five small mushrooms growing on them. I was going to donate my pants to the local

my underpants

museum, but when Mum found them, she said
they were a health hazard and threw them in
the bin.

My bottom hurts and I can't sit down. Please
tell me I have broken the record.

Yours sincerely
Danny Baker

PS My football team beat
Whelley St Peter's five-nil
on Saturday. We've won
the league! We've also
got the Penleydale Cup
Final coming up. I'm the
goalkeeper.

PPS My dad is Bobby Baker. He's got
a certificate from you, for being the Best
Goalkeeper in the World Ever.

ARE YOU A RECORD
BREAKER ?

Dear Danny

207 spots on one bottom is a fantastic attempt.
However, I'm afraid your bottom is not a
world-beater. The Spottiest Bottom in the
World belongs to Thelma McCurdie of Kissimmee,
Florida, USA. On 4 December 1993, a doctor
appointed by the Great Big Book of World
Records counted 11,319 spots on her bottom.
Thelma also holds the record for the Biggest
Bottom in the world. She has a

bottom that an elephant
would be proud to own,
measuring a humongous
622 cm in diameter. I have
included a photograph so
that you know what you
are up against.

Thelma's bottom ↑

25

I hope you can sit down now. If not, why don't you try to break one of the silliest world records in the Great Big Book, and one of my favourites: Leaning Casually Against a Goalpost While Dressed as a Ponsonby Pork Pie (two years, five months, sixteen days, nine hours, five minutes, and fifty-nine seconds)?

Congratulations on winning the league and good luck in the Cup Final, Danny. You must be very proud to be the son of Bobby Baker. He was a great player.

Best wishes
Eric Bibby
Keeper of the Records

Danny and Matthew sat on the kerb outside
Danny's house, reading Mr Bibby's letter.

'You can't try for the Leaning
Casually Against a Goalpost
While Dressed as a Ponsonby Pork
Pie world record,' complained
Matthew. 'You wouldn't be able to
dive on the ground to save a shot,
and we'd lose every match.'

Danny sighed. 'I know. It's tempting though.'

'You can't, Danny,' pleaded Matthew. 'At least,
don't attempt it next Saturday – it's the Cup Final
and Hogton Growlers are a really good side.'

'Don't worry,' said Danny. 'I want to win the Cup
as much as anyone.'

At that moment, he saw his sister heading
towards them, and she didn't look happy.

'You're fish food, Matthew Mason!'
shrieked Natalie. She stormed down the
street, her face as red as a ripe tomato
with sunburn. 'I've got two-weeks'
detention because of you!'

Matthew looked puzzled. 'Did I get your maths homework wrong?'

'No, you dope!' yelled Natalie. 'You got it right!'

'Er . . . that's good, isn't it?' suggested Matthew.

'No, it's not!' shouted Natalie. 'It was *too* right. My maths teacher knew I hadn't done it! Next time you do my homework, get a couple wrong!' She stomped into the house and slammed the front door shut.

Danny looked like he had just got the best birthday present ever.

Matthew looked like a bad smell had just gone up his nose.

It *had*.

He sniffed the air. 'Can you smell gas?' he asked.

'Can *you*?' asked Danny.

'Yeah. I can smell something really rotten, like boiled cabbage and seaweed and eggs and cheese and drains all mixed together.'

Matthew looked around him, trying to find where the awful pong was coming from. His gaze stopped at Danny's feet.

'It can't be,' he said.

'It is!' said Danny. 'They're ready!'

'When are you going to let them out?'

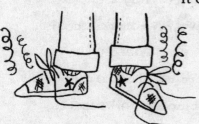

'On Monday in assembly. Take my advice: put a peg on your nose.'

Pong

Dear Mr Bibby

This must be a record! To get myself ready for this attempt, I've been wearing the same pair of socks and shoes every minute of the day and night for the last few months (except when I played football, then I put football socks over the ordinary ones and wore my football boots).

Yesterday I finally took off my shoes during morning assembly. In just under ten seconds, 201 children, five teachers and Mr Rogers the headmaster were unconscious. Nine children and one teacher escaped the pong, because they had very bad colds and their noses were full of snot. My best friend, Matthew Mason, was all right, because I told him to put a peg on his nose. I did the same.

The teacher who escaped called 999.
Firefighters in protective suits and
breathing masks tried to pull my
socks off, but they couldn't do
it. They took me to hospital,
where my socks were cut away
with special surgical scissors. Two
doctors and a nurse passed out. This makes a
total of 210 people who were knocked out by my
smelly feet.

Whiffy sock

Thirty-three of the children who smelt my
feet are still in hospital. The school still stinks
of boiled cabbage and seaweed and eggs and
cheese and drains all mixed together. My feet
look like two pizzas on the end of my legs, and
they smell a bit like pizzas too!

I really hope this is a record, because I am in
Very Big Trouble. The whole football team's out
of action, except for me and Matthew, and
it's the Cup Final on Saturday. So we're going

31

to have to play Hogton Growlers with the nine snotty children who survived my feet. Six of the survivors are girls, none of them even likes football, never mind plays it, and all nine have colds! Four of my new teammates are in Year 1! To top it all, my feet are so sore I can't move properly. We're going to get slaughtered.

Do I have the Smelliest Feet in the world? Please say I do, then at least it will have all been worth it.

Yours sincerely
Danny Baker

PS Here is a photograph of me being taken out of school by the firemen.

(me, going to hospital

The Great Big Book
of World Records
London

Dear Danny

What a *fantastic* effort! I have checked our
records and you are *almost* a record breaker,
but not quite.

The world record for the Smelliest Feet belongs
to Wilma Wallace of Wagga Wagga, Australia. In
December 1987, after a long day of Christmas
shopping in a shopping mall in Sydney, she
kicked off her shoes in the food hall. 217
people were gassed and had to be taken to
hospital. This only just beats the 210 people
affected by *your* feet. Unfortunately, Wilma was
not actually trying to break the world record
so had not taken the precautions you had. She
did not put a peg on her nose. Sadly, Wilma
was killed by her own feet. She was buried in

a lead-lined coffin. To this day, no grass or flowers will grow on her grave, because her feet still pollute the soil.

This terrible story goes to show, once again, how careful you must be when you try to break a world record.

I hope the Cup Final goes better than you expect it to. If not, remember that it could be worse: just think of Wilma Wallace of Wagga Wagga!

Good luck
Eric Bibby
Keeper of the Records

Danny was more fed up than he had ever been in his life. It was the morning of the Final, and he was sat in the kitchen swishing his feet in a bowl of warm water.

Matthew knocked on the back door. 'Is it all right to come in?' he asked, glancing warily at Danny's feet.

'Yeah, they still whiff a bit, but they're not dangerous any more,' replied Danny. 'And we don't have to wear pegs on our noses.'

'How do they feel?' asked Matthew.

'Not bad,' replied Danny. He lifted his feet out of the bowl and began to dab them gently them with a towel. 'I have to bathe them three times a day, but they're still sore. The water in the bowl hasn't gone green for the last two days, and the nurse says that's a good sign. I'm not sure though. I left the bowl in the garden yesterday. Two sparrows took a bath in it and all their tail feathers dropped off!'

'Will you be all right to play today?'

Danny sighed. 'I have to, Matt, but I'm not sure I'll be able to get through the whole game.'

Just then they heard Natalie clomping down the stairs.

'Quick,' whispered Danny, 'Nat's coming. Put the peg on your nose.'

'Why?' asked Matthew as he grabbed a wooden clothes peg from the kitchen table, and pinched it on to the end of his nose.

'Because I haven't let on that she doesn't need it any more,' answered Danny, picking up a peg. 'It's too much fun listening to her speak. And when she eats – *gross*!'

Natalie stomped into the kitchen to get her breakfast, and glared at the boys, but with the peg on her nose, she just looked silly, not scary.

Danny and Matthew giggled.

'Bot's so fuddy?' growled Natalie. She slammed the fridge door shut, and flounced out of the kitchen with her bowl of cornflakes.

The boys collapsed in a fit of laughter.

Outside in the car, Dad sounded the horn to hurry them up.

'Time to go,' said Danny.

In the changing room at Penleydale Town FC, Danny pulled his football boots carefully over his sore feet and laced them up. 'Owww,' he moaned as pain shot through his swollen, tender toes.

The referee opened the door and shouted, 'Teams out on the field, please.'

Danny and Matthew looked at their emergency teammates. The six girls came out from behind a screen at one end of the room, where they had been getting changed. They were giggling.

'These boots are great for tap-dancing,' said Emily Barnes, starting to do a routine in front of the showers.

'They're not taking this seriously, are they?' complained Matthew.

Three of the five-year-olds were kicking a ball to each other. They kept taking huge swings at the ball and missing by a mile.

Danny's shoulders sagged and he frowned at Matthew. 'We don't stand a chance. This is all my fault.'

'You never know, one of the girls might turn out to be the new Pelé,' said Matthew hopefully.

Danny sat down dejectedly on a bench, his head bowed. 'Yeah, right.'

Matthew put his hand on his friend's shoulder. 'There's always next season.'

The Sparrows lined up in the tunnel next to the Hogton Growlers team. Hogton were a big side. They looked at Danny and Matthew, and then at the girls, and then at the little ones at the back, and *then* burst out laughing.

'They should just give us the cup now and save time,' chuckled the Hogton captain.

This is going to be the longest hour of my life, thought Danny.

He hobbled on to the pitch, took up his position in goal and got ready to start the game.

What a Save!

PENLEYDALE SCHOOLS CUP FINAL

Penleydale Schools Cup Final

at

Penleydale Town FC

Three Hills Stadium

Coalclough Sparrows v Hogton Growlers

Sponsored by: Crumbly Crunch Biscuits

TEAMS

Coalclough Sparrows:

1. Danny Baker [Goalkeeper]
2. ~~Jake Dimbleby~~ AMY JOHNSON
3. ~~Tom O'Brian~~ GRACIE GREEN
4. ~~Josh Davis~~ HARRY HOOD
5. Matthew Mason [Captain]

6. ~~James Sedgley~~ KATIE SEDGLEY
7. ~~Jack Dawkins~~ LILY RUSHTON
8. ~~Harry Warburton~~ SOPHIE RUSHTON
9. ~~Sarwit Chudda~~ EMILY BARNES
10. ~~Sam Walters~~ OLIVER HALL
11. ~~Amir Quaiyoom~~ JACK GORDON
12. ~~Ben Prendergast~~ JAMIE LEE

Hogton Growlers:

1. Peter S. Michael [Goalkeeper]
2. Terry Henry
3. Frank Lampoon
4. Steven Gerald
5. Robbie Charlton
6. Paul Schools
7. Kieran Keegan
8. Christian Ronald-Howe
9. David Peckham [Captain]
10. Wayne Mooney
11. Ryan Biggs
12. Alfie Shearer

Hogton kicked off, and in three passes were in Danny's penalty area. The big striker, Wayne Mooney, blasted a fierce shot towards the top corner of the goal.

Danny's smelly feet screamed in agony as he pushed off the ground, but he managed to get his fingertips to the ball and push it over the crossbar.

'Great save, Danny!' shouted Matthew.

From the corner, David Peckham headed the ball down to Danny's left. Danny dropped, and held the ball on the line. The crowd cheered another great save.

The first half went on in exactly the same way: the

Growlers attacking, and Danny making save after save to keep them out. The Hogton goalkeeper didn't touch the ball once in the whole first half.

The referee blew the whistle for half-time. Nil–nil!

Danny got into the changing room and almost collapsed into his seat. He was exhausted.

'Did we win?' asked Amy Johnson.

Matthew ignored her. 'Right, Danny, here's the plan. If you carry on saving everything in the second half, then I'd say there's about a sixteen per cent chance we can win the match on penalties.'

Danny's toxic toes throbbed with pain.

'I can't, Matt. I can't do that again.'

Just then there was a knock at the changing-room door and Danny's dad came in. 'How are your feet?' he asked.

'Terrible,' replied Danny. 'I don't think I'm going to be much use in the second half.'

'Well, whatever happens, I

just wanted you to know that your performance in the first half was the best I've ever seen.'

'Really?'

'Danny, you were fantastic – I couldn't have saved some of those shots. I'm really proud of you.'

'Thanks, Dad.'

Danny didn't feel the pain in his feet when he walked back out on to the field. He could have been walking on feathers.

It's All Over . . .

In the second half, there was nothing Mooney, Ronald-Howe and Peckham could do to beat Danny. But with one minute to go, Wayne Mooney, the Growlers' big striker, got through the defence once more.

Danny moved out to meet him.

The lad had tried to dribble round Danny five times already in the game, but every time Danny had dived bravely at his feet, and picked the ball off his toe. This time Wayne lifted his right foot and blasted the ball towards the goal.

It fizzed past Danny and was heading for the top corner when he somehow arched backwards and managed to touch the ball wide of the post for a corner.

The crowd jumped to their feet and roared and clapped this save, the best one of all. Wayne held his head in his hands.

Danny got up and ran to his goal.

'Come on!' he shouted. 'Everyone back!'

The Growlers' coach screamed at his goalkeeper to go up for the corner, and as the winger took the kick, every other player crowded into Coalclough's penalty area, jostling for position.

It was a good corner kick, arching high and fast into the centre of the area. Danny made his decision and charged off his line, as the Hogton goalkeeper raced forward and leaped high to head the ball. Danny dived and stretched and pulled the ball out of the air with both hands. The Hogton keeper headed nothing, and fell to the ground in a heap. Danny landed on his feet, clutching the ball

tightly to his chest.

Once again the crowd cheered.

'Danny! Shoot!' yelled Matthew.

What's he talking about? thought Danny.

And then he saw it: the empty Hogton goal!

Danny took two steps towards the edge of his penalty area, and with the last bit of strength left in his exhausted legs, punted the ball down the pitch as hard and as high and as straight as he could.

'Owwwww!' His feet had finally had enough. Pain burst up his legs and he collapsed on the grass.

For a moment the whole stadium fell silent. Everyone held their breath. All eyes followed the ball as it looped up high over the halfway line, and then began to fall slowly back to earth. It bounced about fifteen metres inside the Hogton half.

Four of the Growlers team began to race as fast as they could up the field.

The referee chased up the field too, glancing at his stopwatch as the seconds ticked down to the final whistle.

With each bounce the ball got lower and slower, and the four defenders got closer. When it crossed into the Hogton penalty area it was rolling, and they were gaining on it quickly.

The ball trickled over the six-yard line.

The referee looked at his watch again and put the whistle to his lips.

'It's not going to make it,' groaned Danny.

The ball dribbled a metre, then half a metre from the line.

One of the Hogton players was nearly there. He lunged desperately, sliding across the grass towards the ball as it reached the goal line. Danny saw him kick the ball clear, and at the same moment the referee blew his whistle for the end of the game.

The Coalclough supporters shouted, 'GOAL!'

The Hogton supporters yelled, 'NO GOAL!'

'Look!' said Danny, pointing down the pitch. The referee was shaking his head and pointing to his watch. 'It didn't make it.'

'We can still win on penalties,' said Matthew.

Danny groaned quietly. Exhaustion and disappointment rolled over him like a wave. He fell back on the ground and closed his eyes. He had nothing left. He didn't even think he could stand up any more, never mind save five penalties.

Danny just wanted to go to sleep. The howling, bellowing crowd seemed to be a long way away down a deep, dark tunnel.

Suddenly, Danny was being lifted off the ground. He struggled to open his eyes, expecting to see the Coalclough Sparrows'

49

trainers putting him on a stretcher, but there were no trainers and there was no stretcher. He was being carried by people from the crowd, and they were smiling and cheering.

Matthew pushed through the crush of legs and bodies.

'What's going on, Matt?' whispered Danny.

'It *was* a goal!' cried his friend. 'Someone took a video of it and showed the referee. Their player cleared it *after* it crossed the line, and *before* the ref blew the whistle!'

'What?' Danny was groggy and confused.

'WE'VE WON THE CUP!' screamed Matthew.

Two of the Coalclough fans lifted Danny on to their shoulders, and the crowd roared. As they carried him around the pitch, people slapped him on the back and clapped and cheered. Even the girls in the team were dancing with excitement.

'*Now* have we won?' asked Amy Johnson.

'I'm not sure,' answered Gracie Green. 'I think so.'

As the throng of people reached the stand, Danny looked for his mum and dad. He saw them hugging each other and jumping up and down. Mum blew Danny a kiss and Dad punched the air.

And there, on a small table on the pitch in front of the stand, glinting in the sunlight, was the Penleydale Schools Cup.

'Ace!' cried Danny.

'Cool,' agreed Matthew.

Danny Baker - Record Breaker

Dear Mr Bibby

I believe you know my son, Danny Baker. He tells me that he has written to you several times about his world-record attempts.

Yesterday, Danny won the Penleydale Schools Cup single-handedly. I made a video of the game and have enclosed a copy with this letter. During the game Danny made eighty-seven saves that would have been goals for

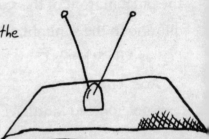

Hogton Growlers, the opposition team. Is this
a record?

Yours sincerely
Robert Baker

PS Danny doesn't know I have sent this, so
if he has not broken a record, can you write
back to me and not tell him. He would be
very disappointed.

The Great Big Book
of World Records
London

ARE YOU A RECORD
BREAKER?

Dear Danny

Congratulations on winning the Penleydale
Schools Cup! Your dad sent me a video of
the game. It was a thrilling match and your
performance was heroic. What a goal! What
brilliant saves!

I counted that you made eighty-seven saves in
the match. I am thrilled to tell you that this
beats the previous world record of fifty-six
saves, held by Robert 'Bobby' Baker, who I am
sure you would agree was the Best Goalkeeper
in the World Ever. I am delighted to enclose
your certificate to record this amazing
achievement.

Put your poor feet up, Danny, and have a rest.

They, and you, have earned it. You are a record breaker!

Best wishes
Eric Bibby
Keeper of the Records

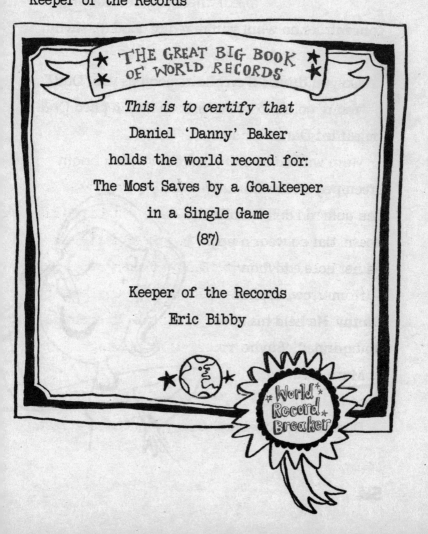

★★ THE GREAT BIG BOOK ★★
OF WORLD RECORDS

This is to certify that
Daniel 'Danny' Baker
holds the world record for:
The Most Saves by a Goalkeeper
in a Single Game
(87)

Keeper of the Records
Eric Bibby

World
Record
Breaker

Danny put the certificate on the wall of his bedroom.

'That's the first of many, Danny,' said his dad. 'Are you going to stop trying to break these silly records and concentrate on what you're really good at: saving goals?'

'Do you think I'll *ever* be as good as you, Dad?'

'You're going to be *better* than me,' replied Dad. He ruffled Danny's hair.

Mum walked into the bedroom with a bright green peg on her nose. 'Wed are you goin' do dell Datalie she doesn' daf do wear a peg od her dose eddybore?'

'Tomorrow,' replied Danny. He held his nose and grinned. 'Baybe.'

Mum laughed. 'Good. Dis ids fud.'

Dad glanced down

at several sheets of writing paper on the bedside table. On the top sheet, Danny had written the words I MUST NOT ATTEMPT TO BREAK WORLD RECORDS IN SCHOOL.

'What's this?' he asked.

'Mr Rogers gave me a hundred lines for letting out my smelly feet in assembly,' explained Danny.

'Ah, well, a hundred's not too many.'

No, thought Danny. A hundred's not enough! There's a record to be broken!

The Baffled
Brain Boffins

WARNING!
SHOPPING WITH
MUM CAN DAMAGE
YOUR HEALTH

Wonderfluff

I must not attempt to break world records in school.
I must not attempt to break world records in school.
I must not attempt to break world records in school.
I must not attempt to break world records in school.
I must not attempt to break world records in school.
I must not attempt to break world records in school.
I must not attempt to break world records in school.
I must not attempt to break world records in school.
I must not attempt to break world records in school.
I must not attempt to break world records in school.
I must not attempt to break world records in school.
I must not attempt to break world records in school.
I must not attempt to break world records in school.
I must not attempt to break world records in school.
I must not attempt to break world records in school.
I must not attempt to break world records in school.
I must not attempt to break world records in school.
I must not attempt to break world records in school.
I must not attempt to bre

To the Keeper of the Records
The Great Big Book of World Records
London

Dear Mr Bibby

My headmaster, Mr Rogers, was a bit cross
about my attempt to break the Smelliest Feet
record. The teachers who had to go to hospital
weren't very happy either. The school has been
disinfected three times and *still* stinks of boiled
cabbage and seaweed and eggs and cheese and
drains all mixed together. Mr Rogers punished me
by making me do one hundred lines, but I kept
on writing. I did 161½ before he caught me. He
got cross about that too, and ordered me do two
thousand lines saying I MUST NOT DO MORE LINES
THAN THE NUMBER OF LINES I'VE BEEN GIVEN.

I didn't have time to finish them at school, but
I kept going at home and managed to do 1,793
before my pen ran out of ink. I'd have done
even more, but my sister Natalie caught me

borrowing her Class Prefect pen. She was cross that I'd tricked her into wearing a peg on her nose after the smelly feet attempt, and she told my mum. Then Mum got cross, because I was supposed to be clearing out the junk under my bed. No one understands what you have to give up to be a record breaker.

I've sent all my lines with this letter. Is this a world record? I hope so, because I'm in trouble with everyone, except my best friend Matthew. He understands. And he likes counting the lines for me.

Yours sincerely
Danny Baker

PS I'm trying to break the Walking Backwards record, but I keep falling over. My bottom's purple and green and yellow and black all over with bruises. Mum said I've got to sit on a big bag of frozen peas. I've also got massive scabs on both elbows. Ace!

The Great Big Book
of World Records
London

Dear Danny

ARE YOU A RECORD
BREAKER ?

Thank you for writing to me again. Your attempt
to break the world record for Punishment
Line Writing fell well short of the mark. You
would have to be incredibly badly behaved to
beat William Archibald Naughtie-McGhie, of
Tillicoultry in Scotland. He was Naughtie by
name, and naughty by nature. William's long
history of naughtiness started when he was
eight years old, but by the time he left school,
he had written a total of 15,201 lines.

Here's how he did it:

He let off a stink bomb in class: 600 lines.
He placed a whoopee cushion on the geography
    teacher's seat: 400 lines.

He hid an enormous furry spider in a bag of
carrots - just as the dinner lady was about
to peel them: 400 lines.

He put paint in the caretaker's mop bucket:
700 lines.

He sprinkled itching powder on the toilet paper
in the girl's washroom: 1,000 lines.

He rearranged all the school library books out
of alphabetical order: 200 lines.

He pulled an ugly face in the class photo:
200 lines.

He glued every chair to the classroom floor:
500 lines.

He wore his clothes back to front, and convinced
the school nurse that his head was on
backwards: 300 lines.

He put cold custard in the teachers' coat
pockets: 500 lines.

He put salt in the sugar shakers, and sugar in
the salt shakers: 400 lines.

He farted in the presence of the Queen during a
royal visit to the school: 5,000 lines.

He blamed the fart on the headmaster:
  5,001 lines.

William was grounded for a month for this
last crime, and having to write so many lines
finally made him stop his naughty pranks.
William Archibald Naughtie-McGhie is now grown
up, and is a police inspector in Aberdeen.

I'm sorry to disappoint you, Danny.

Best wishes
Eric Bibby
Keeper of the Records

PS Be careful walking backwards, Danny. The
Persistent Reverse Perambulation record is a
difficult and potentially dangerous one to
break.

Mum pulled her car into a parking space outside the Wyz Byz supermarket. Natalie, Danny's older sister, slid out of the back

door and stood by the car, grumpy and unhappy, with her arms folded and her shoulders slumped.

Danny climbed out backwards and stumbled straight into her.

'Mum!' whined Natalie, yanking Danny's ear. 'Tell him to stop treading on my toes!'

'Mum!' complained Danny. 'Tell Nat to stop pulling my ears off!'

'Behave yourselves, both of you!' snapped Mum.

Natalie got back in the car. 'I'm staying here,' she announced. 'It's embarrassing going anywhere with him walking backwards all the time, and dressed like *that*.'

Danny and Matthew had made a contraption out of a wire coat hanger, a couple of shin-guards

and the wing mirrors off Dad's old
motorbike. It was strapped to Danny's
shoulders with a pair of his
grandad's braces, so that he
could see where he was going
in the mirrors when he was
walking backwards. He had a
cushion strapped tightly to his
behind with a bright red and
yellow snake belt, to protect his sore bottom.

'I *need* this outfit to help me break the world
record for Persistent Reverse Perambulation,'
protested Danny.

Mum growled and headed for the supermarket
entrance.

As soon as they got inside, Danny backed into
the stack of blue baskets by the door.

'Sorry, Mum. I wasn't looking in my mirrors.'

Mum glared at Danny as he bumped into an old
lady's shopping trolley.

'I *do* apologize,' said Mum. 'He's trying to break
a record.'

'Trying to break his neck, more like,' grumbled the old lady.

Mum grabbed Danny's shoulder and guided him down the aisle.

'Hold on to my trolley,' she ordered. 'And don't let go.'

Danny did as he was told. Mum threw a few cans of Spaghetti Footballs into the trolley

and marched off. She was going so quickly up and down the aisles that Danny struggled to keep up with her. They rounded a corner into the baby-care aisle, and Mum stopped so suddenly that Danny nearly fell over.

'What on earth . . . ? Danny, look at this!'

Danny peered into his mirrors, and saw a three-metre high inflatable baby, wearing a gigantic plastic nappy.

'Ace! That's Baby Ben Bradshaw of Biggleswade, the Wonderfluff Nappy Tot off the TV ads,' said Danny. 'I wonder if that's the biggest blow-up baby in the world? It could be a record breaker.'

'Don't start, Danny,' warned Mum.

'Sorry. Can I go down to the magazine section?' he asked. 'I want to see if me or Dad have got a mention in the latest issue of *It's a Save! The Goalkeeper's Monthly*.'

Mum looked doubtful.

'I'll be careful, honest,' promised Danny.

Mum sighed. 'Yes, go on then.'

He took two steps back from the shopping trolley and crashed into Baby Ben Bradshaw of Biggleswade. As they collided, and the giant balloon baby bounced upwards, Danny tried to grab it without turning round and ruining his record attempt, but he only managed to push Baby Ben higher in the air.

Danny glanced in one of his rear-view mirrors and watched in horror as . . .

. . . the baby wobbled gently upwards, and nudged a mound of toilet rolls . . .

. . . the mound of toilet rolls tumbled, and smashed into cartons of eggs . . .

. . . the eggs flew – splat! – on to the Cornflakes . . .

. . . the Cornflakes bashed the Barleybricks . . .

. . . the Barleybricks pushed the Brancrisps . . .

. . . the Brancrisps bumped the Sugardrops . . .

. . . the Sugardrops toppled a tower of toffee tins . . .

. . . the toffee tins rolled into
a pyramid of melons . . .

. . . the pyramid collapsed
and the melons hurtled like loose
bowling balls into rows of fizzy-cola
bottles, sending them swirling and
whirling and twirling into the air.

'Look out, Mum!' yelled Danny, pushing
her behind a display of lemon-puff biscuits.

The plastic cola bottles smacked on to the ground
and the fizzy liquid inside was so shaken up that
the tops exploded from them like bullets.

By now the Wonderfluff baby had come back
down to earth. It lay on its hands and knees with
its enormous inflated rump sticking up in the
air, being peppered by
bottle tops. They made
a pleasant
drumming
sound on the
big blow-up
nappy, until

suddenly there was a loud 'BANG'!

Baby Ben Bradshaw of Biggleswade, the Wonderfluff Nappy Tot, quivered and shuddered. Then, with a huge roaring whistling fart, took off into the air above Danny and his mum.

The jet-propelled baby whistled and swooped around the Wyz Byz store, knocking over more displays and ripping signs from the ceiling.

'Mum!' shrieked Danny as blow-up Baby Ben banked and looped over the frozen-fish cabinet and went fizzing directly towards her.

All thoughts of his record gone, Danny turned around and raced towards his mother. She stood transfixed and terrified as the giant plastic infant charged at her like an angry bull. At that moment Danny's world went into slow motion. His head throbbed with the sound of his own thumping heartbeat and the horrible whine of the monster baby's squealing fart.

The rocketing inflatable skimmed the puff pastry . . . shaved the nose-hair trimmers . . . brushed the cotton-wool balls . . . and closed in on his mum. With one final despairing effort Danny launched himself upwards, his body arching gracefully into the air as though reaching to save a penalty in the top corner of his goal. He stretched and pushed the baby-shaped missile away from his mum and up towards the roof.

The impact smashed Danny into a pile of giant-sized Wonderfluff nappy boxes, and the whole lot crashed down on top of him.

Everything went black.

Gobbledegook

Danny opened his eyes and looked around. He was in a strange bed, surrounded by flashing, beeping, whirring instruments. There was a woman nearby dressed in a pale blue uniform, with white clogs on her feet. She was writing in a file of papers.

Danny guessed that he was in hospital.

He was tremendously thirsty and asked the nurse for a glass of water. 'My cardigan is full of holes, earwax,' he croaked.

The nurse looked up from the papers. 'You're awake.' She smiled.

'Gumboots, Bobbin,' replied Danny.

The nurse frowned.

'How do you feel, young man?'

Danny licked his parched lips and tried to ask

again for a drink. 'My cardigan is full of holes, earwax,' he repeated.

'Is it?' answered the nurse. She looked puzzled. 'You were bumped on the head by a giant box of Wonderfluff nappies. Do you have a headache?'

Danny shook his head. 'Beep, Bobbin,' he replied. 'But the blue kangaroo is tired and my cardigan *is* full of holes.'

'Er . . . of course it is,' said the nurse, and scurried out of the room.

She returned a minute later accompanied by a small, smiling doctor.

'Hello, Danny.'

Danny held his hand up in greeting. 'Bucket scoops, Wobble,' he replied.

The doctor raised his eyebrows.

'My name's Doctor Gururangan, but you can call me Doctor Sri. How are you feeling?'

Danny mimed drinking, and said, 'My cardigan is full of holes.'

'Would you like a glass of water?' asked Dr Sri, filling one from a nearby jug.

'Gumboots, earwax!' exclaimed Danny.

He gulped the water thirstily. 'Saddlebags,' he said as he rubbed his mouth with the back of his hand.

Dr Sri flashed a light into each of Danny's eyes. 'Do you remember what happened to you?' he asked.

'Gumboots, Wobble,' answered Danny, nodding. 'The blob pickled the plum basket and the treetops threw pies at a wombat.'

The doctor and nurse glanced at each other.

'I've never seen anything like this before,' admitted Dr Sri.

He picked up the red telephone and pressed four numbers. After a moment he said, 'Professor Walkinshaw, would you come down straight away and examine Danny Baker? I know it's very rare, but I think we may have a case of Trauma-induced Nonsensical Pronouncements.'

When the professor ambled into the room, he

wasn't at all what Danny was expecting. He had untidy hair and long, curly mutton-chop whiskers. Under his crumpled white coat he wore an old tartan shirt, baggy blue trousers and cowboy boots. For some reason, Professor Walkinshaw reminded Danny of his grandad's favourite comfy old chair.

'Hi, Danny.'

'Bucket scoops, Wobble.'

'How are you doing, young man?'

'My ears can see daisies.'

'Interesting,' murmured the professor. He turned to the nurse. 'Have you had *any* sense from Danny?'

'None, Professor. He's been talking complete gobbledegook since he woke up.'

The professor rubbed his chin. 'This *can* happen when patients wake in a strange place. Danny might begin to talk normally when he sees something familiar.'

'Danny's family and his best friend Matthew Mason are waiting outside,' suggested the nurse.

'OK, show them in and let's give it a try,' said Professor Walkinshaw.

Danny's mum raced in and kissed and hugged Danny tightly. His dad ruffled Danny's hair.

'Bucket scoops, Beans on Toast,' said Danny. He smiled at Natalie. 'Bucket scoops, Dopey.'

Matthew stood by the door and gave him the thumbs up.

Danny grinned at his best friend. 'Wonderfluff!'

Mum frowned. 'Danny, what are you talking about?'

'Snowflakes burnt my banjo, Beans!'

Mum and Dad looked at each other anxiously, and then at the doctors. 'We don't understand. What's the matter with him?'

'I'm afraid Danny has a severe case of Trauma-induced Nonsensical Pronouncements,' answered the professor.

Dr Sri smiled at Danny's mum and dad. 'What

the professor means is that the blow on the head has made Danny talk gibberish.'

Natalie snorted. 'Danny always talks gibberish – how can you tell the difference?'

'Dribble on the fat bucket, Dopey,' replied her brother.

'I was hoping that it was a mere case of Temporary Acute Vocabulary Disorientation Syndrome,' said the professor. 'But obviously it's more serious than that.'

'Unfortunately, seeing your familiar faces hasn't cured him,' explained Dr Sri. 'But don't worry, if anyone can make Danny well again, it's Professor Walkinshaw. He's the world's leading expert on baffling illnesses.'

'Nothing's beaten me so far,' confirmed the professor.

'So he will get better?' asked Mum.

'I hope so, Mrs Baker, but I can't promise. You may never understand another word Danny says to you, ever again.'

'Tootle on the turtle, Bernard?' asked Danny.

'Yeah, I'm OK, Dan,' replied Matthew. 'How're you?'

'Our tadpole licks a carrot. Are your drumsticks marching up my nose?'

Matthew rummaged in his pocket and pulled out a half-eaten bar of chocolate. 'This is all I've got,' he said, 'but you can have it if you want.'

'Wonderfluff!'

'Just a minute,' interrupted Professor Walkinshaw, gazing at Matthew. 'Can you understand what Danny is saying?'

'Yeah, course I can,' answered Matthew. 'He just said he was starving and did I have anything nice to eat.'

Danny nodded and looked at his mum. 'The worms are cooking tea cosies in the cup.'

Matthew laughed. 'He said he's glad the giant farting baby didn't hurt you.'

'So what did he mean by "Dribble on the fat

bucket, Dopey"?' asked Natalie.

Matthew glanced cheekily at Danny. 'Er . . . he said that you're looking extremely beautiful today, Natalie.'

The boys sniggered. Natalie glared at them.

'This is even more baffling,' said the professor. 'The *Extraordinary Understanding* of Trauma-induced Nonsensical Pronouncements is even rarer than Trauma-induced Nonsensical Pronouncements itself.'

Matthew looked at Danny and rolled his eyes. 'You're a trillion times easier to understand than *him*,' he said.

'Wonderfluff!' laughed Danny.

'Cool!' agreed Matthew.

The Baffling Children

Bucket scoops, Captain Barnacle

All's well now bouncing Bernard can whistle at a box of toenails. She's a lid off a daffodil with trumpets, but she's got loops on a drainpipe to hoot! Sticky-tape buns climbed a feathery broom for bits and bobs of Ace delight, but fairies strum the droop.

Hey diddle diddle, Bernard winks merrily at the dishcloths of doom.

My wobbles die happy. The widgets swoon and Bernard can swing my trainers to fly through the ears of camels. Doggies sing for droopy drawers! Wonderfluff!

Can three coughing spacemen drip whiskers on the Fingers of Gloop? The petals cut through the beans and juggled with a pair of buttery bats, then prancing angels dazzled the piles of withering toads, daring the pots to swish their mangles: purple hippos, purple llamas, purple lions or purple elephants. Oink!

What do piglets find so funny, when mummies do the tango?

Ding-dong
Drainy Babbler

Hello, Mr Bibby

My best friend Matthew will translate this
letter for you. I'm writing
gobbledegook at the moment,
and I'm talking gobbledegook as
well. I was hit on the head by
a great big box of Wonderfluff
nappies, and now I keep talking
rubbish.

The weird thing is, Matthew can
understand everything I say.

The doctors are baffled. They've asked Matthew
to stay at the hospital too, so that he can
tell them what I'm saying. We're both getting
to miss school! Ace!

Remember how I was trying to break the
record for Walking Backwards? I had to stop
to save my mum from being bashed by a big

HUGE
baby

blow-up baby, but I know exactly how long I walked backwards for, because the accident broke my watch: thirteen days, thirteen hours, thirteen minutes and thirteen seconds. Spooky!

Did I break the record as well as my watch?

SPOOKY!

13

Best wishes
Danny Baker

'Bucket scoops', Danny and Matthew

I'm sorry to hear about your accident with
the box of nappies, Danny, but I'm glad to see
your illness hasn't affected your interest in
breaking records.

The World Record for Persistent Reverse
Perambulation is held by Billy Walklater of
Ambleside, Cumbria. He took walking backwards
into the twenty-first century when he began
using satellite navigation to guide him along.
Unfortunately, after 332 days of Reverse
Perambulation, his satnav took him down a dead
end, and he walked backwards into a brick wall.

Billy had broken the record, but his attempt
was over. So he decided to make the most of
the situation and go for the world record for
Standing Against a Brick Wall. He has been
there for 421 days so far, but has another 2965
days to go to before he can claim that record.

Get well soon, Danny!

Ding-dong
Eric Bibby
Keeper of the Records

Professor Walkinshaw and Dr Sri stood by Danny's bed.

'Danny, I've contacted my fellow Brain Boffins around the world to tell them about you, and they're *very* excited. You and Matthew are unique, and they all want to meet you.'

'Snip-snap,' remarked Danny.

'That's nice,' said Matthew.

'I'd like you both to spend a few days on the Bertha Blenkinsop Ward, so that we can study you and try to make you better, Danny.'

'It's where all the other children with baffling illnesses stay.' Dr Sri smiled. 'It's got a really good games room.'

Bertha Blenkinsop Ward

'Helping those with baffling illnesses...'

'Wonderfluff!' said Danny. 'Clean that tricky zebra and keep the garden small.'

'Yeah,' agreed Matthew. 'Let's hope there *are* some kids our age to play with.'

At the door to the ward, Dr Sri stopped and pulled a false beard out of his pocket. It was short

and black. He hooked the ends over his ears, and carefully arranged the beard close to his chin.

He reached into a small box by the door, and pulled out two more beards. He handed a long, curly orange one to Danny, and a thick, bushy brown one to Matthew.

'Will you put these on, please?' he said.

'Why?' asked Matthew.

Dr Sri smiled. 'You'll see.'

He led them down the corridor towards three nurses who were standing by the reception desk. They were wearing false beards too. One of them strolled over to the boys.

'I'm Sister Morris,' she said,

'and you must be Danny and Matthew.'

She showed them into the games room, where a boy and girl sat in front of a screen, using handsets to control two brightly coloured racing cars speeding around a track. The boy was also wearing a false beard.

'Bucket scoops!' called Danny.

'That means "Hello",' said Matthew. 'Danny's started to talk gobbledegook, and only I can understand him. That's why we're here. I'm Matthew, by the way.'

'Hi, my name's Alex,' said the boy, 'and this is Abigail.'

'What time's the doorknob?' asked Danny.

'What's wrong with you?' translated Matthew.

'Well, my bottom turns blue whenever I eat a banana,' replied Alex.

'And my ears began to buzz when my dad grew

a beard,' said Abigail. 'Listen.'

Danny and Matthew leaned close to Abigail. Her ears were buzzing softly, as if each one had a small bee trapped inside it.

'Wonderfluff!' breathed Danny.

'Cool,' agreed Matthew. 'Why aren't *you* wearing a false beard?' he asked Abigail.

'Because I'm the reason everyone's wearing them in the first place,' she explained. 'Professor Walkinshaw is hoping I'll be cured if I get used to the sight of them.'

'Has it worked?' asked Matthew.

'It's starting to,' answered  Abigail. She reached for a small square black box that hung around her neck on a strip of pink ribbon. 'This is a sound-level meter. The reading's getting lower and lower all the time. You should have heard the noise when it began. My ears sounded like racing cars!'

Danny laughed. 'Wonderfluff!' His tummy rumbled. 'Why did you shovel coal on a mongoose?' he asked. 'Cream crackers!'

Alex and Abigail looked at Matthew.

'That means, "When do we have lunch? I'm starving!"'

'In about half an hour,' replied Alex. 'But don't get excited, the food here *stinks*. You're lucky it's not Friday, or you'd be getting stinky fish.'

'Yeah, *and* beans and sprouts and cabbage,' complained Abigail.

Matthew pulled a face.

'Gross.'

'It's great fuel for farts though,' commented Alex. 'On Fridays we can all trump for England.'

Danny's eyes lit up as an idea popped into his head.

'Tip-tap the moonbeams, because kittens bob their heads to tubas,' he said.

Matthew frowned. 'What are you up to, Danny?'

Alex and Abigail looked puzzled.

'What did he say?' asked Alex.

'This Friday, every kid in the hospital must hang on to their trumps,' explained Matthew.

'Why?' giggled Abigail.

'Walnuts are skating down the rug because their noses are like train sets,' babbled Danny. 'Snooker cue.'

Matthew grinned. 'We're going to try and break the world record for the Loudest Trump – pass it on.'

'How do we dollop cat-food on the light bulbs of smooth?!' Danny asked.

Alex and Abigail turned to Matthew. 'Why trump for England when we can trump for the world?!'

Shock Tactics

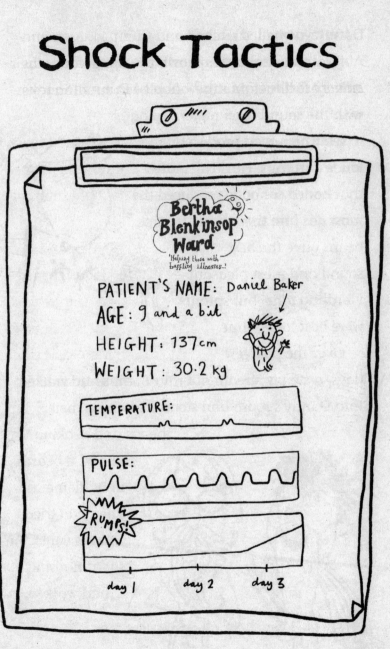

Danny yawned, stretched and trumped. Alex and Abigail were right: this horrible hospital food was *brilliant* fart fuel. Matthew had been running tests with the sound-level meter, trying to see which food produced the loudest trumps. He'd calculated that boiled cabbage produced the most gas and the longest trumps, beans gave the best sound and most pleasant vibrating tone, but sprouts were best for volume.

Over the past few days, a steady stream of Brain Boffins had walked into Danny's room and stood scratching their heads and stroking their false beards in bafflement. They had tried various cures, but so far nothing had worked.

They had talked to Danny in his own style of gobbledegook.

'Tie up the egg roll and fan a broom socket,' said the professor.

'I've tussled with tumbleweed on a damp and dusty bee,' pronounced Dr Sri.

'Flip a goalpost sandwich,' exclaimed Sister Morris.

Danny stared at them. 'Snitch the crumpets, bar none,' he said.

'What a load of rubbish,' translated Matthew.

Danny woke up one morning and there was a huge cardboard cut-out of Baby Ben Bradshaw staring down at him from the end of  his bed. He jumped in fright, but it didn't cure him.

Neither did being tapped
gently on the head for an
hour with a Wonderfluff
nappy.

Danny got out
of bed and put on his
dressing gown. He shuffled sleepily
down the ward towards the games room.
He opened the door and jumped back in shock.

The room was crammed with children, doctors
and nurses. Danny's mum
and dad, and Matthew's
mum and dad were there
too, along with Natalie
and Matthew, Alex and
Abigail. Everyone (apart
from Abigail), was wearing
a false beard, but what
astonished Danny most was
that every single person in the
room was wearing a supersized
Wonderfluff nappy over the

top of their normal clothes.

Danny shook his head as if trying to shake the sight from his eyes.

They all stared back at him, silent and hopeful.

'Well?' asked Mum anxiously.

Danny rolled his eyes. 'Are the watering cans woozy because there's a singing kipper in my trouser pocket?' he asked.

Everyone in the room groaned with disappointment.

Matthew grinned. 'No, Dan, we're not all wearing nappies because we had the hospital curry last night. The Boffins thought the sight of everyone wearing a nappy would cure you.'

Danny glanced at Natalie and chuckled. 'Why smudge Dopey when you can elbow the bursting bubbles?' he asked.

Matthew laughed. 'You're right, Dan, she does look a total twit!'

Natalie's face turned crimson. She ripped her nappy off and hurled it to the floor. 'You are going to be *so* sorry about this!' she growled at the boys

as she stomped out of the games room.

'Nappies off, everyone,' called Dr Sri.

Professor Walkinshaw sighed heavily. 'The Sudden Visual-trigger Sensory-overload Resolution has failed,' he announced. '*I've* failed.'

'This is the most baffling case I've ever seen,' one of the Brain Boffins commented. 'We need more brains on this one.'

The professor nodded thoughtfully. 'I'm going to call every Baffleologist in the world. We'll have a symposium, and Danny and Matthew will be the stars of the show!'

The Mighty Trump

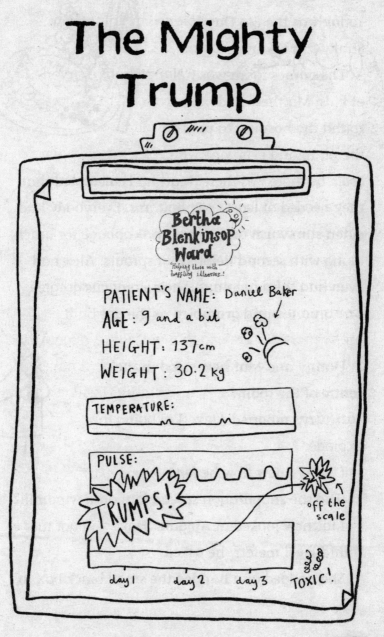

Bertha Blenkinsop Ward

Helping those with baffling illnesses..!

PATIENT'S NAME: Daniel Baker

AGE: 9 and a bit

HEIGHT: 137cm

WEIGHT: 30.2 kg

TEMPERATURE:

PULSE:

TRUMPS!

off the scale

day 1   day 2   day 3   TOXIC!

Today was the Big Day: Stinky-fish Friday.

The games room was full of kids. Matthew had been round the hospital to pass on the plan, and everyone who *could* be there *was* there. Matt had calculated that they needed at least sixty bottoms. Everybody had eaten stinky fish and beans and cabbage for lunch, along with second helpings of sprouts. Alex had even had third helpings. Their stomachs gurgled and groaned and grumbled as the gas built up.

Danny and Matthew stood in the centre of the room.

'Hurry,' moaned Alex. 'I'm going to explode.'

Danny knew how he felt.

'Did the snapdragon spread jam on a windmill?'

Matthew looked at Abigail. 'Have you got the sound-level meter?' he asked.

She nodded and handed the small black box to

Matthew. 'Actually, I don't need it any more,' she admitted. 'My ears stopped buzzing completely yesterday when I saw all those beards. I didn't tell them I was cured though, because they'd have sent me home and I'd have missed the Trump.'

Matthew placed the sound-level meter in the centre of the room.

'Drop a bread bin up the stairs and brush the scooter,' Danny told Matthew. 'Tall tigers wrestle with a jelly flea and watch the pink rabbits "boom!".'

'Everyone bend over and point your bottoms at the meter,' Matthew instructed. 'Danny'll count to three – sorry, I mean "flea" – and when he says "boom!" let rip!'

The kids put their fingers in their ears and bowed low.

Danny shouted, 'Bun . . . glue . . . flea . . . boom!'

As one, they blew out the built-up gas. It was a humongous, growling, roaring trump. It

was a trump
so loud and
ferocious that
the windows in

the room shattered, the
television exploded, a
water pipe burst, picture

frames crashed off the
wall, chairs clattered over,
books toppled from bookshelves,
the light in the room began to
flicker, and everybody's false
beards flew off.

'Tickle my flowerpots!'
exclaimed Danny.

Professor Walkinshaw
and Dr Sri hurried into the
room and stared at the
devastation.

'What's that
terrible smell?' asked
Dr Sri, holding his nose.

'Was it a gas leak?'

'Was it an earthquake?' yelled the professor.

'It was a trump,' explained Matthew.

'Something happened to my bottom!' cried Alex, looking shocked.

'And mine!' laughed Matthew, holding his behind and wiggling. 'It was a ripper!'

'No, I mean something else, something . . . *strange*.'

Alex picked up a banana from the floor, where it had been blown out of the fruit bowl by the force of the trump. He peeled it, took a big bite and swallowed. After a moment, he dropped his trousers and glanced over his shoulder. Everyone stared at Alex's bottom, and his bottom stared back at them, pink and rosy. It hadn't turned blue!

The professor was thrilled. 'Heavens to Betsy!'

he exclaimed. 'He's been cured! This is all thanks to you, Danny! Accidental Flatulence-induced Symptom Resolution is unheard of!'

Dr Sri translated, 'He means that this is the first time anyone has been accidentally cured by a trump.'

'Wonderfluff!' exclaimed Danny.

The professor stroked his false beard thoughtfully. 'It could be the loudness or the force of the trump that produced the resolution,' he said. 'But I suspect that the precise mixture of chemicals in the trump gas reacted with the blue in Alex's bottom and turned it pink.'

'We need to analyse it quickly, before it disappears,' said Dr Sri.

Danny's tummy rumbled. 'Peel the flutey bugle, Wobble, and dangle a lollypop!' he laughed.

'Don't worry, Doctor, there's plenty more where that came from!' Matthew translated.

'Bernard, is the octopus melting on the

skateboard?' Danny asked him.

His friend went over to the sound-level meter and looked at the reading. 'We got a hundred and ninteen point nine decibels.'

'The grass-green mole was the pick of the chocolate cans.'

'Yeah, you're right, Danny, that *must* be a record,' agreed Matthew. 'Should we get writing to Mr Bibby?'

'Gumboots!' Danny grinned.

The Stars of the Show

St Egbert's Children's Hospital, Walchester

Bucket scoops, Captain Barnacle

I'm Drainy boots. Our carpets go moo, and bouncing Bernard rumbles merrily in his coffee-pot, for better or worms.

The lemony handbags pickled on your tram tracks and saw deep wallows of tinkling lilac troops. An aeroplane shook a snowball, but it wouldn't shake for Drainy. When penguins waddled on woozy tops, lava lamps waltzed on an itchy gumboil and couldn't slurp in a fusspot. Warty diggers snuggle-up bumps! Did the whatnot rasp a nippy biscuit?

Ding-dong
Drainy Babbler

Hello, Mr Bibby

It's Danny again. I'm still talking nonsense, so my best friend Matthew will tell you what I'm saying, like last time.

Yesterday, sixty-seven of the kids at the hospital produced a trump that measured 119.9 decibels. It cured our new friend Alex, but it didn't cure me. After the damage the trump caused, the hospital says it is never going to serve stinky fish and beans and sprouts and cabbage on a Friday ever again. The kids say I'm a hero! Was our trump a world-beater?

TRUMP!

s-t-i-n-k-y cabbage

Best wishes
Danny Baker

trump

Dear Danny and Matthew

Bad luck again! You and your friends blew just
short of the record. A couple more sprouts might
have made all the difference.

The Loudest Single Trump ever recorded was
measured at 121.4 decibels. It was produced
by the Woolloomooloo Didgeridoo rugby team
on 14 July 1996 during a tour of Tonga. Like
you, they had been fuelled by a special diet
- stinky fish, spinach, cabbage, pumpkin and
bananas. At a banquet held in their honour, on
a signal from their captain Hayden Blow, the
whole team broke wind simultaneously in front
of King Taufa-ahau Tupou IV.

The team broke the Trump Decibel world record,

but offended the king and his people so much that they were asked to leave Tonga and never return.

I hope you put your fingers in your ears when you trumped. 119.9 decibels is about as loud as a jet aircraft taking off, but I don't suppose I need to tell *you* that!

I'm really sorry you're not better yet, Danny, but don't give up hope, there is *always* a cure. As your new friend Alex discovered with your monster trump, the trick is just to find it.

Best wishes
Eric Bibby
Keeper of the Records

Danny stood with Mum, Dad and Matthew outside the Big Hall at the University of Walchester. The room was packed with hundreds of Brain Boffins from all over the world, all there to examine Danny and Matthew.

Dad ruffled Danny's hair.

'How do you feel, Dan?'

'GB.'

Mum put her arm around Danny's shoulders.

'Are you sure? You seem a bit fed up to me.'

Danny shrugged. 'The clock is full of wobbles and custard, Beans,' he explained. 'The cat can smile for ants and a spoon can ring its socks.'

Mum looked at Matthew.

'I don't want to baffle doctors any more, Mum,' Matthew translated. 'It was fun for a while, but now I want to be normal again.'

Inside the hall, Danny heard Professor Walkinshaw announce

to the hundreds of assembled Brain Boffins, 'Ladies and gentlemen, may I introduce the most baffling case I have ever seen: Danny Baker and his best friend Matthew Mason.'

For the next hour Danny and Matthew told their story and answered questions in their uniquely baffling way. At the end of the session the boys walked off the stage to deafening cheers and clapping.

Mum gave Danny a hug.

Dad shook Matthew's hand.

'Well done, both of you,' said Dad.

'It's a bookworm, Toast,' sighed Danny. 'Do dancing spots worry a dinosaur's boots? Because the cows on bicycles have tea-bag toes.'

Matthew frowned and translated, 'I'm a bit fed up, Dad. Do you think I'll ever be able to speak normally again? All I can look forward to are loads more tests.'

Mum knelt down and looked at Danny. She was smiling.

'There *is* something else to look forward to,' she

said. 'I've got some news that will cheer you up.'

'Turnip?' asked Danny.

'What?' asked Matthew.

'I'm going to have a baby,' Mum said.

Danny's jaw dropped. He felt as
though his breath had got stuck
in his chest. He couldn't get air in
or out. He made several choking
sounds.

'Danny . . . ?' said Mum
anxiously.

Danny tried with all his might to
force the air out of his throat. It burst
out in a rush of words.

'Whatdoyoumeanyouaregoingtohaveababy?' he
blurted.

'What do you mean, you are going to have a
baby?' Matthew translated.

'What?' asked Dad.

'What?' asked Mum.

'He said, "What do you mean, you are going to
have a baby?"' repeated Matthew.

'I *know* that's what he said!' shouted Mum.

'Danny!' yelled Dad. 'I think you're cured! Say something else.'

'Fidget on a corner flag, Beans on Toast.'

Mum, Dad and Matthew gasped.

Danny laughed. 'Just kidding!'

At that moment, Professor Walkinshaw walked off the stage.

'Danny, Matthew, you've baffled the world of Boffindom,' he beamed. 'But don't worry, I promise we *will* find a cure.'

'It's OK, Professor, I've just had an Out-of-the-blue Mum-delivered Baby-news Gobbledegook Cure,' announced Danny.

The professor frowned. 'What?' he asked.

'His mum's going to have a baby,' Matthew translated. 'And Danny can talk normally again.'

'Ace!' said Danny.

'Don't you mean Wonderfluff?' laughed Matthew.

Danny Baker - Record Breaker

Dear Mr Bibby

baffled
BRAIN

This is me writing! Guess what? The only person talking gobbledegook now is my doctor, Professor Walkinshaw. He says I've had a 'Resolution by Unexpected Announcement of Impending Sibling Arrival'. In other words, I'm cured!

Just before my mum told me she was going to have a baby, me and Matthew managed to baffle 1,327 Brain Boffins from all over the world. The professor said that in all his years as the world's leading Baffleologist, he'd never known so many big-brained Brain Boffins to be baffled at one time. Does this mean we're world-beaters?

Best wishes
Danny

The Great Big Book
of World Records
London

ARE YOU A RECORD
BREAKER ?

Dear Danny

This is wonderful news! I was very worried
about you and I am so relieved you are
better. It's also great to hear about your
truly outstanding display of Boffin-baffling.
Congratulations! I can confirm that you and
Matthew have broken the world record for
Tandem Simultaneous Baffling of Big-brained
Brain Boffins.

I have enclosed two certificates, one for each of
you.

Your letter arrived just in time. I leave
today for Lake Chargoggagoggmanchaugga-
goggchaubunagungamaugg, near the town of
Webster, Massachusetts. It has the longest place

name in America, and has more letter 'g's than any other word in the world.

.

The name of the lake means something like 'Englishmen at Manchaug at the fishing place at the boundary'. The townspeople are hoping to gather at least 2,461 Englishmen at the fishing place at the boundary, to break the previous record. I am going to count how many Englishmen turn up and, as an Englishman myself, take part in the attempt.

With luck, Danny, this time next week, I could be a record breaker too!

Well done to both of you.

Best wishes
Eric Bibby
Keeper of the Records

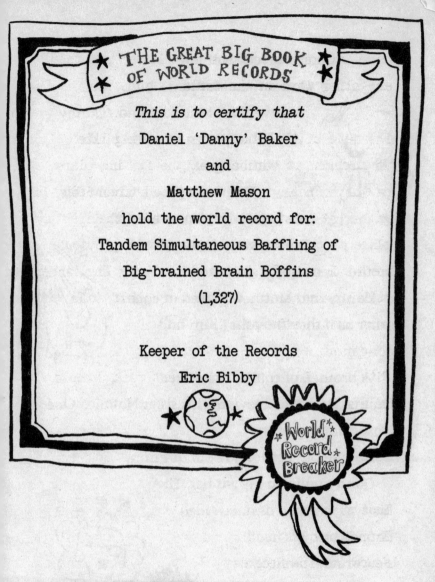

THE GREAT BIG BOOK OF WORLD RECORDS

This is to certify that

Daniel 'Danny' Baker

and

Matthew Mason

hold the world record for:

Tandem Simultaneous Baffling of

Big-brained Brain Boffins

(1,327)

Keeper of the Records

Eric Bibby

World Record Breaker

Danny and Matthew stared at their certificates.

'Ace,' said Danny.

'Cool,' agreed Matthew.

Dad ruffled Matthew's hair. 'You deserve that, Matt,' he said. 'Danny would have been in a real pickle without you.'

Mum sat at the kitchen table, fixing the broken toaster. 'So, Danny, would you prefer a brother or a sister?' she asked.

Danny and Matthew looked at each other as if they thought Mum had gone mad.

'A brother, of course!' answered Danny. He nodded towards his sister Natalie. 'One Nasty Nat's enough!'

Natalie put her tongue out at him.

Danny pulled a face at her. Then his eyes widened as a new idea popped into his head.

'I wonder what the world record is for the Stinkiest Nappy?'

Glossary of Danny Baker's Gobbledegook

Bucket scoops – Hello

Ding-dong – Best wishes

Gumboots – Yes

Beep – No

Earwax – Please

Saddlebags – Thank you

Wobble – Doctor

Bobbin – Nurse

Beans – Mum

Toast – Dad

Bernard – Matthew

Drainy Babbler – Danny Baker

Captain Barnacle – Mr Bibby

Dopey – Natalie

GB – OK

Wonderfluff! – Ace!

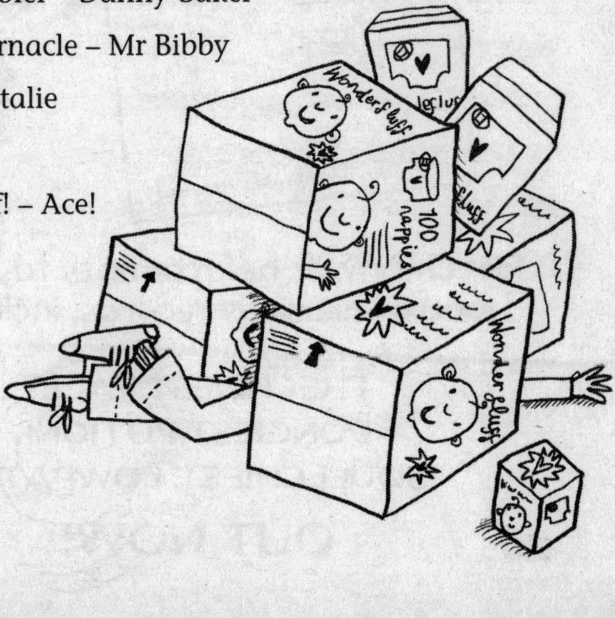

THE WORLD'S
AWESOMEST AIR-BARF

STEVE HARTLEY

TO THE MANAGER
The Great Big Book
of World Records
London

Dear Sir,
I flew to Spain yesterday
and I filled thirteen sick-bags
on the flight. Mum says it was all
the cola and cheese and pickle
sandwiches I had at the airport.
She's right – that's why I had them!
Is this even close to breaking the
record for filling sick-bags? If it's
not, I'll try again on the way home.

Yours faithfully,

Danny Baker

(Aged nine and a half)

WARNING!
NOT TO BE
READ AT
MEALTIMES

Join Danny as he attempts to smash a
load of hilarious records, including:

FRECKLIEST FACE!
PONGIEST POTION!
SQUELCHIEST COWPATS!

OUT NOW!